G·L·O·B·E
LITERATURE

Language Enrichment Workbook

Globe Book Company
Englewood Cliffs, New Jersey

PURPLE LEVEL

Printed in the United States of America   10   9   8   7   6   5   4   3   2   1

ISBN: 1-55675-198-2

GLOBE BOOK COMPANY
A Division of Simon & Schuster
Englewood Cliffs, New Jersey

Love Letter

Recall and Sequencing

Put the following events in the order that they happened in the story, "Love Letter."

_____ **1.** Jake goes to the graveyard and finds Helen's grave.

_____ **2.** Jake finds his old stamps from his childhood.

_____ **3.** Jake takes his first letter to Wistal postal station.

_____ **4.** Jake buys a desk.

_____ **5.** Jake goes on a date.

_____ **6.** Jake discovers the first letter.

_____ **7.** Jake finds the old house where Helen lived.

_____ **8.** Jake finds the old picture of Helen.

_____ **9.** Jake goes to the library to look at books about when Helen lived.

_____ **10.** Helen answers Jake's letter.

First Person Demonstrative

Part I. Hyperbole

Hyperbole is creating an image by exaggeration. Use hyperbole to create such an image for each of the following. Use the phrases at the bottom of page 3.

tiny dog

The dog _____

_____

It was _____

_____

hot day

crying child

The child cried _____
over the broken toy.

She was so tall her head _____
_____

tall woman

| touched the clouds | buckets of tears |
| as hot as an oven | no bigger than a mouse |

First Person Demonstrative

Part II. Similes

Similes are comparisons between two things using the words *like* and *as*. Through the comparison, a particular characteristic or feeling is highlighted and an image is created.

The following are all similes. Choose the most suitable ending to create the simile. Place the letter in the space supplied.

_____	**1.** Mary swims	a.	as a bear
_____	**2.** Susie sings	b.	light as a feather
_____	**3.** The swimming pool is	c.	like a fish
_____	**4.** Her hair is as black	d.	as a picture
_____	**5.** She is as thin	e.	as a bullet
_____	**6.** The cake is as	f.	like an angel
_____	**7.** Paul is as hungry	g.	cold as ice
_____	**8.** The baby is as quiet	h.	as coal
_____	**9.** Marty is as fast	i.	as a stick
_____	**10.** Mary is as pretty	j.	as a mouse

First Person Demonstrative

Part III. Imagery through Similes

Create an image using **similes**. Write a simile to describe each of the illustrations. The first one is done for you. Work with a partner. You may want to use some of the images at the bottom of page 6.

two cars colliding

_____

_____

_____

_____

thunderstorm

freeway traffic

_____

_____

_____

_____

waterfall

| explosion | volcano |
| children playing | thousands of ants |

What is Once Loved Spring

Part I. Contractions

Match each phrase with the proper contraction.

_____	**1.** do not	a.	can't
_____	**2.** will not	b.	he's
_____	**3.** I will	c.	they'll
_____	**4.** she will	d.	I'll
_____	**5.** he will	e.	don't
_____	**6.** they will	f.	aren't
_____	**7.** I am	g.	we're
_____	**8.** you are	h.	she'll
_____	**9.** he is	i.	I'm
_____	**10.** we are	j.	won't
_____	**11.** she is	k.	isn't
_____	**12.** they are	l.	you're
_____	**13.** are not	m.	they're
_____	**14.** is not	n.	he'll
_____	**15.** can not	o.	she's

Write a complete sentence using the given contraction.

I'm _____

she'll _____

you're _____

won't _____

we're _____

they're _____

What is Once Loved Spring

Part II. Personification and Hyperbole

Personification and hyperbole are both figures of speech.

Personification occurs when we give human characteristics to animals or objects. **Hyperbole** is exaggeration.

Identify the following sentences as either personification or hyperbole. Place a P for personification or an H for hyperbole in the space provided.

_____   **1.** The chair squeaked in protest.

_____   **2.** The wind cried all night long.

_____   **3.** I'm so tried; I could sleep for a week.

_____   **4.** As I opened the door, the cold slapped me in the face.

_____   **5.** I'll die if I can't go to the dance.

_____   **6.** The brakes screamed as he tried to avoid the fallen tree.

_____   **7.** The waves nipped at her ankles.

_____   **8.** She lost her head and dashed between the cars.

_____   **9.** Sadness lives in that house.

_____   **10.** We walked a million miles to the movies.

Up On Fong Mountain

Part I. Homophones

The following are pairs of homophones. **Homophones** are words that sound alike but have different spellings and different meanings. Write sentences for each of the pairs to show that you understand the difference.

1. capital — capitol

2. weather — whether

3. route — root

4. red — read

5. their — there

6. hear — here

7. tale — tail

8. peace — piece

1. _____

_____

2. _____

_____

3. _____

_____

4. _____

_____

5. _____

_____

6. _____

_____

7. _____

_____

8. _____

_____

Up On Fong Mountain

Part II. Root Words

The following words contain **root words**. These are the basic words from which other words are formed. Find the root word and write it on the line next to the word. Use a dictionary if you need help.

desperately _____

ambitious _____

construction _____

consideration _____

whimsical _____

seriousness _____

natural _____

foolish _____

Write a complete sentence for each given word.

desperately _____

_____

ambitious _____

_____

whimsical _____

_____

natural _____

_____

foolish _____

_____

construction _____

_____

Up On Fong Mountain

Part III. Vocabulary

Complete the following sentences about the story, "Up On Fong Mountain," by filling in the blanks with words from the Word Bank.

WORD BANK

way	shop	journal
argue	donut	comes
parking	winks	shop
orders	argue	break-up
Mom	assigns	ancestors
job	sneakers	donut

1. Miss Durmacher _____ the _____ project.

2. Brian Marchant _____ at Jessie.

3. Brian and Jessie _____ about Brian's _____ .

4. Brian and Jessie _____ about Brian always having to have his own _____ .

5. Brian and Jessie _____ .

6. Jessie gets a _____ at Dippin Donuts.

7. Jessie's _____ comes into the donut _____ .

8. BD _____ to the _____ shop.

9. BD throws his _____ into the _____ lot.

10. Mrs. Richmondi _____ BD out of the _____ shop.

Romeo and Juliet

Archaic Vocabulary

Ten archaic words and their definitions are listed below. Write a sentence using each word.

Tis — it is

foul — dirty

thou — you

knave — serving boy

nay — no

portly — heavy

ay — yes

doff — take off

cell — small room

ere — before

_____

_____

_____

_____

_____

_____

_____

_____

_____

_____

_____

Grey Day Here-Hold My Hand Finis

Part I. Similes and Metaphors

Similes are the comparison of two things by using the words *like* or *as*. Example: The boy was as happy as a clam.

Metaphors are comparisons of two things without using the words *like* or *as*. Example: Her hands are a book of her life.

Identify the following sentences as either similes or metaphors. Place an S for a simile or an M for a metaphor in the space provided.

_____ 1. The tired child was like a bear going into hibernation.

_____ 2. Trick-or-treating children are busy bees.

_____ 3. John is an encyclopedia of information.

_____ 4. The cars looked like ants from the top of the skyscraper.

_____ 5. The classroom was as silent as snowfall.

_____ 6. The traffic is a nightmare.

_____ 7. You are a prince for helping.

_____ 8. Elisabeth's mind is like a hothouse of flowers.

_____ 9. Her eyesight is like that of an eagle.

_____ 10. Paul is a soldier ant.

Pick one metaphor from above and write a sentence describing the image created. For example, why would someone say "Her hands are a book of her life"? What characteristics do hands and books have in common?

_____

_____

Grey Day Hold My Hand Finis

Part II. Senses

Name the five senses. _____

Fill in the missing words in each sentence. Circle the words that pertain to the senses. Then write each circled word and the sense it is associated with.

The rose was _____ as velvet and

_____ like perfume. It _____ in the sunlight.

_____

_____

_____

The puppy_____ at the door. He

_____ like a string mop in the rain and

_____ like a wet sponge.

_____

_____

_____

The cake _____ to be a mountain of chocolate and _____ like the corner bakery in the morning. It _____ in your mouth.

_____

_____

_____

Think about a trip you have made. Using the five senses, write a paragraph describing your journey.

_____

_____

_____

_____

_____

_____

_____

_____

_____

_____

Housecleaning Where Have You Gone?

Slang

Slang is an informal vocabulary unique to a particular group or region. "Far out" is a slang term used by some youngsters to mean very good. Slang is used sometimes to show you belong to the group that uses it.

List ten slang terms and write your own definition. The first one has been done for you.

1. radical   – terrific
2. _____
3. _____
4. _____
5. _____
6. _____
7. _____
8. _____
9. _____
10. _____

Define slang in your own words. _____

_____

Does slang have a use? _____

_____

Should you always use slang? _____

_____

When should you use slang? _____

_____

Where are You Now, William Shakespeare?

Part I. Homophones

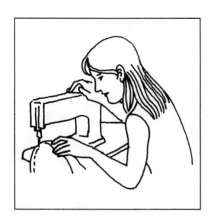

Homophones sound alike but are different in meaning and spelling. Use each of the homophones listed below in a sentence showing that you understand the differences.

to, two, too
sew, so, sow
tow, toe
air, heir

1. _____
2. _____
3. _____
4. _____
5. _____
6. _____
7. _____
8. _____
9. _____
10. _____
11. _____

Name _____   Date _____

Where are you Now, William Shakespeare?

Part II. Recalling the Plot

1. Marijane's girlfriend was named _____

   _____

2. Marijane's first boyfriend was named _____

   _____

3. Marijane was happiest wearing _____

   _____

4. Marijane's father was her _____.

5. Marijane's girlfriend had a crush on a movie

   star named _____.

6. Marijane had a crush on some movie stars whose

   names were _____, _____

   and _____.

7. Marijane and her girlfriend argued about _____

   _____

8. _____ heard from Ronald Reagan first and received an _____.

9. _____ was jealous of Ronald Reagan.

10. A simple way for Marijane to please her father would be to wear a

    _____ and _____.

Who is your favorite movie star? Describe some of the movies he or
she has done and the reasons why you like him or her.

_____

_____

_____

_____

_____

_____

I Dream a World Reflections

Synonyms

Synonyms are words which have similar meanings. Match the synonyms.

_____	**1.** hungry	a.	car
_____	**2.** depressed	b.	awful
_____	**3.** amazement	c.	swollen
_____	**4.** diner	d.	odd
_____	**5.** cocoa	e.	get along
_____	**6.** unusual	f.	junk
_____	**7.** picky	g.	mirror
_____	**8.** bloated	h.	starving
_____	**9.** reflector	i.	hard
_____	**10.** adhere	j.	coffee shop
_____	**11.** garbage	k.	astonishment
_____	**12.** problem	l.	particular
_____	**13.** smile	m.	group
_____	**14.** difficult	n.	couch
_____	**15.** horrible	o.	hot chocolate
_____	**16.** bunch	p.	sad
_____	**17.** cooperate	q.	difficulty
_____	**18.** hesitant	r.	grin
_____	**19.** sofa	s.	stick
_____	**20.** automobile	t.	unsure

Use five of the above words in original sentences.

_____

_____

_____

_____

Name _____   Date _____

Appointment in Bagdad

I. What image comes to mind when you hear the name of the
capital, Iraq, Bagdad? What kinds of buildings do you imagine?
What clothes do the people wear? In the space below, draw that
image.

```
┌─────────────────────────────────────────────────────┐
│                                                       │
│                                                       │
│                                                       │
│                                                       │
└─────────────────────────────────────────────────────┘
```

II. Write a few sentences to describe your picture.

_____

_____

_____

_____

III. Illustrate what you think "Death" looks like. Describe your
picture with a short paragraph.

IV. Write a few sentences to describe your
drawing of Death.

_____

_____

_____

_____

_____

_____

Appointment in Bagdad

Illustrate what you think "Death" looks like. What color clothes is "Death" wearing? Is "Death" fat or thin? Beautiful or ugly? Describe your picture in a short paragraph.

Write your sentences here.

_____

_____

_____

_____

Appointment at Noon

Can you unscramble the following sentences from "Appointment at Noon" so that they make sense? The first one has been done for you.

1. brought visitor She the back.

   _____

2. wall at He glanced the clock.

   _____

3. a He for moment thought.

   _____

4. quite He seemed sincere.

   _____

5. chair a gave She him.

   _____

6. door kept eyes his He on the.

   _____

7. heard I said You what.

   _____

Appointment at Noon

Can you write the sentences on the preceding page so that they are in the order they happened in the story? (You may want to refer to the story to help you.)

1. _____

   _____

2. _____

   _____

3. _____

   _____

4. _____

   _____

5. _____

   _____

Incident in a Rose Garden

Make a list of ten common nouns that appear in the poem "Incident in a Rose Garden." Then alphabetize your list.

NOUNS	ALPHABETICAL ORDER
1. _____	_____
2. _____	_____
3. _____	_____
4. _____	_____
5. _____	_____
6. _____	_____
7. _____	_____
8. _____	_____
9. _____	_____
10. _____	_____

Boy in the Shadows

Write sentences using four of the following vocabulary words related to the story: Ozarks, thicket, haggard, listlessly, finicky. Can you use all five of the words?

_____

_____

_____

_____

_____

_____

_____

Boy in the Shadows

ADJECTIVES are words that describe a person, place, thing, or idea. See if you can think of some adjectives to describe Jayse from the story "Boy in the Shadows." Write them.

Use three of your adjectives in a sentence that describes Jayse.

_____

_____

_____

_____

Boy in the Shadows

Find the main ideas of the paragraphs that follow. Write them in the spaces provided.

1. paragraphs 3 and 4 on the first page of the story

_____

_____

_____

_____

2. paragraph 1 on the third page of the story

_____

_____

_____

_____

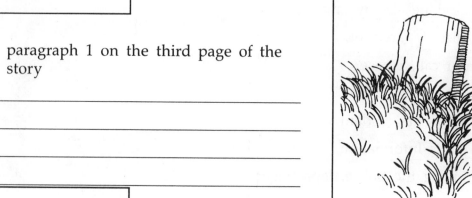

3. paragraph 2 on the sixth page of the story

_____

_____

_____

_____

Sorry, Wrong Number

Write S if the words form a sentence; write NS if they do not form a sentence.

_____ **1.** Hello, George.

_____ **2.** Where are you now?

_____ **3.** How awful!

_____ **4.** While telephoning.

_____ **5.** Depends on what.

_____ **6.** Isn't it obvious?

_____ **7.** The murder hasn't been committed yet.

_____ **8.** Don't worry.

_____ **9.** I'm alone all day and night.

_____ **10.** Police department, Precinct 43.

_____ **11.** Your call, please?

_____ **12.** Is this Plaza 4-2295?

_____ **13.** That is all, madam.

_____ **14.** This is Information.

_____ **15.** Ringing the police department.

_____ **16.** Telephones are funny things.

_____ **17.** Now, why did I do that?

_____ **18.** Check it!

_____ **19.** For the night.

_____ **20.** Duffy speaking.

Sorry, Wrong Number

The PREFIX "tele" comes from the Greek language and means "far" or "distant." Some English words that use this prefix are: telephone, telegraph, telecast, telephoto, telescope, telegram, telethon, and television.

Try to place the letter of the word next to its meaning. Look for clues in the definitions to help you.

___d___   **1.** telegraph

_____   **2.** telephone

_____   **3.** telephoto

_____   **4.** television

_____   **5.** telescope

_____   **6.** telecast

_____   **7.** telethon

_____   **8.** telegram

a. a machine that shows visual images or programs

b. a television broadcast

c. an instrument used to see objects out of the normal scope

d. a system that uses codes to communicate

e. a long television program used to raise money

f. a machine used to talk to someone far away

g. a written message sent by a telegraph

h. a picture or photograph of a distant object

Sorry, Wrong Number

Make sentences of your own using these vocabulary words from the story "Sorry, Wrong Number."

1. client- _____

2. specific- _____

3. invalid- _____

4. drastic- _____

5. vague- _____

6. inefficient- _____

7. exclusive- _____

8. coincidence- _____

9. entitled- _____

10. civic- _____

Thus I Refute Beelzy

A suffix is a group of letters added to the end of a "root" word which gives the word a slightly different meaning. Here are some examples of suffixes which have been added to root words.

SUFFIX	NEW WORD
-ly	1. sadly
-ful, -ness	2. thoughtfulness
-er	3. nicer
-est	4. greatest
-ship	5. friendship

Find the root words above and use each in your own sentence.

e.g. 1. ROOT WORD: _sad_____

SENTENCE: _The hungry dog looked so sad._____

2. ROOT WORD: _____

SENTENCE: _____

3. ROOT WORD: _____

SENTENCE: _____

4. ROOT WORD: _____

SENTENCE: _____

5. ROOT WORD: _____

SENTENCE: _____

Thus I Refute Beelzy

A prefix is a group of letters added to the beginning of a "root" word which gives the word a different meaning. Here are some examples of prefixes and the new words formed by adding them to a root word.

PREFIX	MEANING	NEW WORD
un-	opposite of	unhappy
pre-	before	precooked
dis-	not	dissatisfied
post-	after	postgame
super-	more than	supermarket

Now, make up 10 sentences of your own using the root word and the new word formed when a prefix is added.

e.g. 1. ___The boy was happy to see his father._____

2. ___The mother is unhappy because it is so cold._____

3. _____

4. _____

5. _____

6. _____

7. _____

8. _____

9. _____

10. _____

hist, whist

RHYMING words sound alike. The title words of the poem "hist, whist" rhyme. Some other words that rhyme are *nose* and *rose*; *man* and *fan*; *blue* and *shoe*. Circle the words below that rhyme with the word at the top of the column. When you are done, see if you can be a poet and add two more lines of your own to the ones at the bottom of the page! Choose words from this sheet.

MOON	TIME	FUNNY	CANDY
book	rhyme	bunny	fan
June	lime	sunny	dandy
moose	pie	honey	band
tune	tile	money	sandy

Having candy
Sure is dandy,

_____

_____

Overheard on a Saltmarsh

Words that sound alike but have different spellings and meanings
are called homonyms. Some examples are: hair, hare; rain, reign; to,
two, and too; pair, pear, and pare. Find the word that is a homo-
nym of:

1. stare _____   6. be _____

2. no _____   7. which _____

3. reeds _____   8. there _____

4. lie _____   9. blew _____

5. fair _____   10. plane _____

RHYMING

Draw a line from the word on the left to its rhyming word on the
right. (Example; stair and care)

moon	teen
so	kite
green	neighbor
daughter	talked
night	souls
labor	plain
walked	soon
rolls	taught
brought	blow
crane	water

Of Missing Persons

Antonyms

An antonym of a word means the opposite. For example, "tall" is the opposite, or antonym, of "short." Draw a line from the word on the left to its antonym on the right.

upstairs	right
inside	always
arrived	young
old	bright
left	nothing
easy	departed
dark	awake
everything	outside
asleep	difficult
never	downstairs

Now use some of these words in sentences.

e.g. This is not the left glove. It is the right one!

_____

_____

_____

_____

_____

Of Missing Persons

Synonyms

A synonym of a word means the same. For example, "big" is the same, or is a synonym of, "large." Draw a line from the word on the left to its synonym on the right.

sick	frightened
scared	slender
doctor	sea
thin	small
talk	right
shut	ill
little	all
correct	physician
everything	close
ocean	discuss

How many of these synonyms can you use in sentences? Can you use two of them in one sentence? Try it!

_____

_____

_____

_____

_____

The Listeners

SINGULAR NOUNS name *one* person, place, thing, or idea. PLURAL NOUNS name *more than one* person, place, thing, or idea. To make most nouns plural, just add -s or -es. An example is *pencil/pencils*. When a noun ends in y and is pronounced like the letter i, change the y to i before adding -es. An example is *fly/ flies*.

Below are twelve singular nouns. See if you can write the plural form of each noun. Remember to change the y to i in "sky" and "cry."

SINGULAR NOUN	PLURAL NOUN
1. door	doors
2. floor	
3. house	
4. moonbeam	
5. stair	
6. hall	
7. call	
8. cry	
9. horse	
10. heart	
11. voice	
12. sky	

Eldorado

Look through the poem "Eldorado" for a word that rhymes with each of the following. Write it in the space next to the word. Do you know any other words that rhyme? Write those down too. Use the second blank space for your own rhyming words.

night: _____   _____

bold: _____   _____

long: _____   _____

replied: _____   _____

found: _____   _____

he: _____   _____

soon: _____   _____

strength: _____   _____

hide: _____   _____

blew: _____   _____

The Loch Ness Monster

Draw a picture of what you think the monster looks like. Write a short description of your monster. It is ugly? Is it friendly? What does it do?

My Monster
_____

_____
_____
_____
_____
_____
_____

The Loch Ness Monster

Write some sentences using the following vocabulary words from "The Loch Ness Monster": forests, mountainsides, farms, traveler, glens, caravans, and acre.

_____

_____

_____

_____

_____

_____

_____

_____

On the Path of the Poltergeist

State the main ideas of the paragraphs that follow. Write them in the spaces provided.

1. paragraph 4 on the first page of the story

_____

_____

_____

2. paragraphs 2 and 3 on the second page of the story

_____

_____

_____

3. paragraph 3 on the third page of the story

_____

_____

_____

The Getaway

Compound Words

A COMPOUND WORD is a word made from two smaller words. Some examples of compound words are: something, made from the words some and thing; anywhere, made from the words any and where. Use the words below to form compound words. Choose from Column A for the beginning of the word, and from Column B for the ending of the word. (You may use a word more than once.) Write the compound words on the lines below.

COLUMN A	COLUMN B
get	thing
some	where
turn	away
under	one
any	ever
when	road
far	driver
screw	stand
zig	paper
news	off
rail	zag
out	side

_____ _____ _____

_____ _____ _____

_____ _____ _____

_____ _____ _____

_____ _____ _____

The Getaway

Synonyms

A SYNONYM is a word that means the same as another word. An example is "big" and "large." Find a word below that means the same as a word in the word bank. Write the synonym next to a word below.

1. lucky- _____
2. main- _____
3. moaned- _____
4. twinkling- _____
5. gleam- _____
6. suspense- _____
7. divide- _____
8. conclude- _____
9. glanced- _____
10. startled- _____

shine
frightened
fortunate
end
separate
groaned
sparkling
principle
looked
excitement

The Getaway

You End It!

In the story "The Getaway," the robbers were directed to a bridge that doesn't exist. What do you think will happen to the two men? Will the police catch up to them? Will the robbers find a way to cross the river? In the space above, draw a picture of what you think will be the final scene, or outcome of this story. Then write a few sentences to explain the outcome.

Sherlock Holmes

Breaking up Compounds

The words below are all COMPOUND WORDS. On the lines next to each word, write the two smaller words that make the bigger, compound word.

1. dogcart = _____dog_____ + _____cart_____

2. stepfather = _____ + _____

3. nobleman = _____ + _____

4. anyone = _____ + _____

5. sometimes = _____ + _____

6. hallway = _____ + _____

7. goodnight = _____ + _____

8. nightgown = _____ + _____

9 matchbox = _____ + _____

10. neighborhood = _____ + _____

11. afternoon = _____ + _____

12. stepdaughter = _____ + _____

13. breakfast = _____ + _____

14. toothbrush = _____ + _____

15. yourself = _____ + _____

16. outside = _____ + _____

17. fireplace = _____ + _____

18. housekeeper = _____ + _____

19. headache = _____ + _____

Sherlock Holmes

When a story is told in FIRST PERSON, a character in the story describes the events. When a story is told in THIRD PERSON, the author tells about the events, but does not take part in the action. "I climbed a tree" is an example of a sentence written in first person; "The boy climbed a tree" is an example of a sentence written in third person. Read each sentence below. If the sentence is written in first person, write an F before it. If the sentence is written in third person, write a T before it.

__F__   **1.** I'll order coffee, since I see you are shivering.

_____   **2.** The left arm of her jacket had mud spots in places.

_____   **3.** He married my mother in India.

_____   **4.** We had all we needed to be happy.

_____   **5.** They sat for awhile, talking about the wedding.

_____   **6.** Suddenly I heard a scream—a woman's scream.

_____   **7.** Her sister died without speaking again.

_____   **8.** My life became lonelier than ever—until lately.

_____   **9.** He'd heard of Holmes before.

_____   **10.** I never know when I'm safe from him.

_____   **11.** They examined the outside and then the rooms.

_____   **12.** I think it was an excuse to move me from my room.

_____   **13.** This brings up a few problems with my theory.

_____   **14.** He didn't see anything odd.

_____   **15.** She was to use her lamp as a signal to them.

_____   **16.** He didn't see anything unusual.

_____   **17.** Will you pass me some toast, please, Watson?

Sherlock Holmes

Mysteries and detective stories have their own set of special terms or words. Show that you know what each of these detective terms means by using each in a sentence.

1. homicide- _____
   _____

2. assault- _____
   _____

3. coroner- _____
   _____

4. theory- _____
   _____

5. investigation- _____
   _____

Trifles

People who live in different parts of the United States may speak with a different accent and may use different expressions. This language which is particular to a certain region is called a DIALECT. Susan Glaspell, the author of "Trifles," uses dialect to make her story seem more real. Can you match the words and phrases on the left to the standard language shown on the right?

1.	a load of potatoes	**a.**	people
2.	folks	**b.**	don't know
3.	rockin'	**c.**	isn't
4.	ain't	**d.**	get along
5.	pleating at her apron	**e.**	folding her apron
6.	dunno	**f.**	a lot of potatoes
7.	raised 'round here	**g.**	I say
8.	Well, can you beat the woman!	**h.**	rocking
9.	get on	**i.**	Can you believe that?
10.	I declare	**j.**	I suppose it is.
11.	I s'pose 'tis.	**k.**	raised around here
12.	takin'	**l.**	I sleep soundly.
13.	I sleep sound.	**m.**	taking

Trifles

When an ending such as -ed, -ing, -s, or -es is added to a word, then we say that we have added a suffix to the ROOT WORD. In the word "writing," "write" is the root word: "-ing" is the suffix. All of the words below have had suffixes added to them. Can you find the root word in each? Underline it.

bringing	trifles	strangled
happened	snooping	moved
started	feelings	hands
saying	falters	preserves
talked	potatoes	pans
wanted	going	slicked
knocked	shivers	knows
doing	looked	looks
pleated	minded	pulling
laughed	pointed	patches
notified	died	

Now use at least five of the above words in sentences.

_____

_____

_____

_____

_____

Trifles

I am reading a book. The boy is reading a book.

The first sentence above describes the action in the picture in FIRST PERSON. (The writer is involved in the activity.) The second sentence describes the action in THIRD PERSON. (The writer is not involved.) Write a sentence of each type to describe the pictures below.

book/read

FIRST PERSON: _____

_____

THIRD PERSON: _____

_____

bike/ride

FIRST PERSON: _____

_____

THIRD PERSON: _____

_____

school/enter

Rattlesnake Hunt

Suffixes can be added to words to change the meaning of the words. Example: herpetology—the study of reptiles
herpetologist—one who studies reptiles
The suffix -ist has been added. Notice that the y in herpetology was dropped before adding the suffix. Change these words by adding the suffix -ist. Be sure to drop the letter(s) in parentheses.

1. science (ce) = _____

2. geology (y) = _____

3. journal = _____

4. botany (y) = _____

5. chemistry (ry) = _____

6. dental (al) = _____

7. art = _____

8. astrology (y) = _____

9. physics (s) = _____

Choose some of the new words above and use them in sentences.

_____

_____

_____

_____

_____

Rattlesnake Hunt

Have you ever seen a rattlesnake? Have you ever heard it rattle? Do you know why this rattlesnake is called a diamond backed? Picture in your mind a scene from the story "Rattlesnake Hunt." Draw that scene in the space above. Then write a few sentences to describe your illustration.

Earth/Earth

February 23, 1989

Several dry winters and a series of fires are believed to have sent coyotes in record numbers onto Solano County ranchlands in search of prey, according to landowners. Richard Emigh, owner of one of the largest sheep ranches in the area, said coyotes have killed about 60 of his lambs, worth a total of $10,000. County agricultural officials said the animals caused an estimated $44,000 in damage to livestock and equipment in 1986-87, the last period for which figures were available.

When a newspaper reporter gets information for a story, he needs to find out WHO (is the story about), WHAT (happened), WHEN (did the story take place), WHERE (did the story take place), WHY (did it happen), and HOW (did it happen).

Read the newspaper article on this page. Find the WHO, WHEN, WHERE, WHY, and HOW in the story.

WHO? _____

WHAT? _____

WHEN? _____

WHERE? _____

WHY? _____

HOW? _____

The Lady, or the Tiger?

The following words are from the story "The Lady, or the Tiger?"
Can you write each word correctly in the sentences below?

perception
semi   barbaric   subject   tribunal
portals   genial   fair   relentless
reflect   fancies   doleful   station

1. His _____ of the idea was unclear.

2. The wild and cruel man was _____.

3. We entered through the _____.

4. Her imagined _____ were always

   pleasant.

5. The water was _____ -frozen.

6. His _____ in life was a bookkeeper.

7. He was _____ and without pity.

8. She felt _____ and began to cry.

9. He was the king's _____.

10. I began to _____ about the past.

11. My friend has a _____ personality.

   12. The firl's face was _____.

   13. The soldier appeared before the _____ for a

      trial.

      Use one of the words in your own sentence.

      _____

      _____

The Lady, or the Tiger?

Some sentences can be made by combining two smaller sentences.

Example: The cookies had chocolate chips.
         The cookies had pecans.
         The cookies had chocolate chips and pecans.

Sentences can often be combined by using the words and, or, and but. Choose one of these words to form one sentence from each pair of sentences below. The first one has been done for you.

1. His ideas were savage.
His ideas were reckless. _His ideas were savage and reckless._____

2. Men displayed their courage.
Beasts displayed their courage. _____

3. A door beneath him opened.
The accused person stepped out. _____

4. Will he choose the lady?
Will he choose the tiger? _____

5. The king's justice was not only fair.
The king's justice was fast. _____

6. They would witness a bloody slaughter.
They would witness a wedding. _____

7. Gold had brought the secret.
Power had brought the secret. _____

8. Every heart stopped beating.
Every breath was held. _____

9. The student has finished.
The student has done a good job. _____

The Bat/The Bird of Night

Below are SYNONYMS, or words that mean the same, for some of the vocabulary words from the poems "The Bat" and "The Bird of Night." Use the second synonym to create a different sentence from the one in the poem. Write the new sentence.

1. (hook/attach) I hook my hind feet into a wall or ceiling.
   I attach my hind feet to a wall or ceiling. _____

2. (nourishment/food) Sleep is my nourishment.

   _____

3. (devour/eat) I devour tons of insects.

   _____

4. (floating/flying) A shadow is floating through the moonlight.

   _____

5. (bright/colorful) Its beak is bright.

   _____

6. (heaves/moves) All the air
   swells and heaves.

   _____

   _____

Write sentences to describe
pictures A and B.

A. _____

_____

B. _____

_____

A Secret For Two

Below are two paragraphs from the story "a Secret For Two." Can you fill in the blanks with words that makes sense? Choose from these words.

Streets	city	name
large	delivered	Pierre
years	Montreal	horse
white	children	saints
as well		blocks

Montreal is a very large _____city_____. But, like all _____ cities, it has some very small streets. _____, for instance, like Prince Edward Street, which is only four _____ long. No one knew Prince Edward Street _____ as did Pierre Dupin. For _____ had _____ milk to the families on the street for thirty _____ now.

During the past fifteen years, the _____ that drew the milk wagon used by Pierre was a large _____ horse named Joseph. In _____, especially that part of Montreal that is very French, the animals, like _____, are often given the names of _____. When the big white horse first came to the milk company, he didn't have a _____.

A Secret For Two

First, Second . . . and Last

Read the sentences below. Can you put them in the order they appeared in the story "A Secret For Two?" What happened first?

__7__ Pierre is struck by a truck.

_____ Pierre names the white horse.

_____ Pierre refuses to leave his job.

_____ Pierre dies.

_____ Joseph learns the milk route.

_____ The president of the company suggests that Pierre retire.

_____ Joseph dies.

_____ Jacques discovers that Pierre has been blind for five years.

_____ Pierre's mustache turns pure white.

A Secret For Two

A SUMMARY is a shortened form of the important parts in a story. When you tell someone about a movie you've seen, you tell about all of the main elements of the movie. You are giving a summary of the movie. On the lines below, write a short summary of the story "A Secret For Two." Be sure to include only those details that are most important to understanding what the story is about. You may use some of the sentences from the preceding page. Don't forget a title.

_____

_____

_____

_____

_____

_____

_____

_____

_____

_____

_____

_____

Name _____ Date _____

Chee's Daughter

In each of the sentences below a VOCABU-LARY word from the story "Chee's Daughter" has been underlined. Can you match each word with its meaning below? Circle the letter of the word that means the same.

1. After watching the couple, we surmised that they were married.
   a. called   b. planned   c. realized
2. The girl had not combed her hair. It looked straggly.
   a. messy   b. beatiful   c. neat
3. The woman was wearing a collection of rings, necklaces, brace-lets, and bright scarves. She looked gaudy.
   a. elegant   b. overly-dressed   c. dirty
4. The corn was ripe, so the family began to harvest it.
   a. gather   b. throw   c. plant
5. The tourists got off the bus.
   a. friends   b. visitors   c. sheep
6. He had won that argument.
   a. disagreement   b. promise   c. conversation

Chee's Daughter

Adjectives ⟶ Adverbs

An ADJECTIVE is a word that describes a noun. An ADVERB is a word that describes a verb. In the sentence "She has a sweet smile," "sweet" is an adjective describing a smile. In the sentence "She smiled sweetly," "sweetly" is an adverb describing how she smiled. To change *some* adjectives to adverbs, just add the suffix -ly. (sweet—sweetly)

Add -ly to the adjective in parentheses to change it to an adverb that makes sense in the sentence. Write the new word in the blank. The first one has been done for you.

1. (loud) The child screamed _____loudly_____.

2. (calm) Chee tried to speak _____.

3. (quick) Little One _____ ran to her father.

4. (stubborn) Old Man Fat _____ refused to let his granddaughter go.

5. (silent) Chee found it difficult to stand by _____.

6. (bright) The sun shone _____ on the fields.

7. (careful) Chee wanted to approach the situation _____.

8. (suspicious) He knew that he could not act _____.

9. (willing) Little One flew _____ into her father's arms.

10. (quiet) The family worked _____.

11. (kind) The teacher smiled _____ at the student who had finished the workbook page.

Chee's Daughter

Synonyms

unruly	boundary	looked	
confidence	position	clutched	
volumes	injured	tired	desires

Find a word above that means the same as the word or words underlined in the sentences below. Write it in the blank after the sentence.

1. The university library contains 7,000 <u>books</u>. _____.

2. Joan has a lot of <u>faith in herself</u>. _____.

3. John's dog was <u>hard to control</u>. _____.

4. That gate is the <u>border of our property</u>. _____.

5. He had a <u>place on the team</u>. _____.

6. Patrick <u>hurt</u> his leg. _____.

7. Jose <u>wants</u> a pony. _____.

8. The child <u>glanced</u> at his mother. _____.

9. The horse was <u>weary</u> after its journey. _____.

10. Manuel <u>grabbed</u> his coat. _____.

Navaho Chant

Prepositions

PREPOSITIONS are words that tell where, how, when, or why. Look at the words underlined in the sentences below.

a. The dog ran <u>around</u> the yard.
b. The cat ran <u>up</u> the tree.

"Around" and "up" are prepositions that tell where. Choose from the list of prepositions in the box. See if you can correctly write one in each of the sentences below.

to
beside
under
above
from
over
on
in
near
between

1. He ran _____ the window.

2. He hit the ball _____ the net and scored a point.

3. She sat _____ the tree so that she was in the shade.

4. I received a letter _____ my friend.

5. Their new house is _____ the city in a tall building.

6. Planes fly _____ the ground.

7. The pen was _____ the paper.

8. The ball landed _____ my feet and bounced off my toes.

9. He sat _____ us so that we could each sit beside him.

10. He kept a glass of water _____ his bed.

Navajo Chant

Some Silly Syllogisms

A SYLLOGISM is made up of three statements. The first two statements are facts, and the third statement is a conclusion. An example of a syllogism is:

Birds fly.
A bluejay is a bird.
A bluejay flies.

In the syllogisms below, some conclusions are true, but some are false. Read the first two statements and decide whether the third statement, or conclusion, is true or false. Circle the T if the statement is true; circle F if the statement is false.

1. All wheels are round.
   The world is round.
   The world is a wheel.
       T   F

2. All oceans have water.
   The Pacific has water.
   The Pacific is an ocean.
       T   F

3. All languages have words.
   Navajo is a language.
   Navajo has words.
       T   F

4. All houses have doors.
   Cars have doors.
   Cars are houses.
       T   F

5. All Apples have seeds.
   Oranges have seeds.
   An orange is an apple.
       T   F

6. A rock is solid.
   Ice is solid.
   Ice is a rock.
       T   F

7. All planets are round.
   Mars is a planet.
   Mars is round.
       T   F

8. All cats have whiskers.
   Fluffy is a cat.
   Fluffy has whiskers.
       T   F

9. All books have pages.
   TOM SAWYER is a book.
   TOM SAWYER has pages.
       T   F

10. All combs have teeth.
    People have teeth.
    People are combs.
        T   F

The Gold Medal

Syllables not Syllogisms

A SYLLABLE is a part of a word that makes a certain sound or beat. The word "medal" has two syllables. Can you hear them? When a word has a double consonant (i.e. ll, mm etc.), the word is divided into syllables between the two consonants.

    a. sum/mer
    b. val/ ley

Syllabicate the following words:

1. glimmer ___glim/mer___

2. humming _____

3. leggy _____

4. happened _____

5. summoned _____

6. sudden _____

7. swelling _____

8. jutting _____

9. hidden _____

10. really_____

11. happy _____

12. ribbons _____

13. cotton _____

14. mannered _____

15. follow _____

16. funny _____

17. simmer _____

18. muttered _____

19. nodded _____

20. sunny _____

Use at least three of these words in sentences.

_____

_____

_____

The Gold Medal

Adverbs

An ADVERB is a word that describes a verb. In the sentence "The girl ran quickly," "quickly" is an adverb because it describes how the girl ran. Choose from the list of adverbs in the box to complete each sentence below. Write the correct adverb in the blank.

early
often
once
around
slowly
carefully
proudly
loudly
happily
soon

1. The mule plodded _____ down the steep, rocky slope.

2. The bank opened _____, as the sun was rising.

3. The bell will ring _____, since school is almost over.

4. He liked her and _____ called her on the telephone.

5. When he won the prize, he stood _____.

6. She looked _____ for her family.

7. The runners listened _____ to the instructions.

8. The tiger roared _____.

9. The group has only _____ sung together.

10. They lived _____ ever after.

The Gold Medal

You Are the Artist

Use the space to the left to draw a picture of Amanda as her mother saw her.

Use this space to draw a picture of how Mrs. Hawthorne, the old lady who lived on the corner, saw Amanda.

Now draw a picture of Amanda as Mr. Grogan, the grocer saw her.

Finally, draw a picture of Amanda as Chief's owner saw her, and as Amanda saw herself.

Conversation with Myself/Happy Thought

Feelin' Good!

A positive feeling means a good feeling, and a negative feeling means a bad feeling.

Put a P next to each positive feeling and an N next to each negative feeling below.

1. Sick-times you go inside yourself. _____

2. Chastened, I cringe and agree. _____

3. I'm still young and glad. _____

4. I am thinking a happy thought. _____

5. I stick out my tongue. _____

6. I stare unhappily at my face in the mirror. _____

7. I love people. _____

8. I stare at myself demanding "Who am I?" _____

9. She laughed happily. _____

10. I feel that I understand nothing. _____

11. It's slipped from smile to giggle. _____

12. You sit and look outside yourself at people passing by. _____

13. You don't even know. _____

14. This is the last sentence on the page!. _____

Ta-Na-E-Ka

A CONTRACTION is one word made from two words. An apostrophe is used to show where there are missing letters. "Aren't" is a contraction for the words "are not." "Can't" is a contraction for the words "can not."

Change the underlined words below to contractions.

1. I <u>do not</u> want to be a warrior. _____

2. <u>You have</u> gone through it. _____

3. Many <u>did not</u> return. _____

4. <u>You would</u> be a terrible warrior. _____

5. <u>They will</u> be happy to see me. _____

6. <u>You are</u> smart. _____

7. <u>I will</u> tell you again. _____

8. We <u>could not</u> return until the white had worn off. _____

9. <u>Do not</u> call my parents. _____

10. Roger tried to smile, but <u>could not</u>. _____

Ta-Na-E-Ka

Needs

<table>
<tr><td></td><td>

SUPPLIES

raincoat
blanket
knife
tent
mirror
candy bar
gloves
matches
flashlight
bottled water
can opener
toothbrush
hairbrush
sunscreen lotion
socks
perfume
radio
</td></tr>
</table>

You are lost in the forest. Choose the five items you think are *most* important for survival from the list above. List them. Write a sentence telling why you included each item in your list. You can use the sentence pattern: I need a _____ because. . . .

1. _____

2. _____

3. _____

4. _____

5. _____

Dead at Seventeen

What Person are You?

A story told in FIRST PERSON is when a character in the story describes the events. The story will include words such as "me, we, us."

A story told in THIRD PERSON is when a narrator tells about the events without taking part in the action. The story will include words such as "they, he, she."

Read each sentence below. Decide if it is written in first person or third person. Write an F if it is told in first person; write a T if it is told in third person.

1. The day he died was an ordinary school day. _____T_____

2. I saw all my relatives at the funeral. _____

3. She felt very much alone. _____

4. We threw our books in the locker. _____

5. He carried on the tradition. _____

6. I was overwhelmed with grief. _____

7. They wished they had taken the bus. _____

8. He was excited about driving the car. _____

9. He was happy about being his own boss. _____

10. I am glad that I have finished this page. _____

Dead at Seventeen

Changing Person

Agony claws at my mind. I am a statistic. When I first got here I felt very much alone. I was overwhelmed with grief, and I expected to find sympathy.

I found no sympathy. I saw only thousands of others whose bodies were as badly mangled as mine. I was given a number and placed in a category.

The paragraphs above are from the letter titled "Dead at Seventeen." They are written from the author's perspective, and so they are in first person. Rewrite the paragraphs in third person on the lines below. (Remember, third person means that you will tell the story about someone else.) You will need to change the underlined words.

_____

_____

_____

_____

_____

_____

_____

_____

What is the main idea of these two paragraphs?

_____

Thank You, M'am

Being Contrary

ANTONYMS are words that have opposite meanings. An example of two antonyms is GOOD/BAD.

Write the letter of the antonym next to each of the words on the left. Can you supply another antonym of your own to the *'d words?

__l__	*1.	large _little_	a.	up
_____	2.	front	b.	go
_____	3.	push	c.	shout
_____	4.	down	d.	back
_____	5.	give	e.	left
_____	*6.	stop _____	f.	wrong
_____	7.	loose	g.	wet
_____	*8.	whisper _____	h.	pull
_____	9.	right	i.	shut
_____	10.	correct	j.	take
_____	11.	laugh	k.	out
_____	12.	empty	l.	small
_____	13.	dry	m.	tight
_____	*14.	happy _____	n.	over
_____	15.	frown	o.	sad
_____	*16.	open _____	p.	smile
_____	17.	in	q.	full
_____	18.	under	r.	there
_____	19.	here	s.	cry
_____	*20.	hot _____	t.	cold

Thank You, M'am

Synonyms

A SYNONYM is a word that means the same as another word. An example of synonyms is GLAD/HAPPY.

Write the letter of the synonym next to a word on the left. Can you supply a second synonym to the *'d words?

_____	**1.** frail	**a.**	hung
_____	**2.** woman	**b.**	alone
_____	**3.** middle	**c.**	big
_____	**4.** supper	**d.**	let go
_____	**5.** dull	**e.**	soiled
_____	**6.** wild	**f.**	weak
_____	**7.** timidly	**g.**	shyly
_____	***8.** repair _____	**h.**	faith
_____	***9.** large _____	**i.**	horrible
_____	**10.** purse	**j.**	little
_____	**11.** single	**k.**	lady
_____	***12.** dirty _____	**l.**	center
_____	**13.** slung	**m.**	closed
_____	**14.** shake	**n.**	savage
_____	***15.** terrible _____	**o.**	boring
_____	***16.** small _____	**p.**	tremble
_____	**17.** release	**q.**	dinner
_____	**18.** trust	**r.**	correct
_____	**19.** shut	**s.**	handbag
_____	**20.** pause	**t.**	stop

Name

Date

Thank You, M'am

Cause—Effect

A CAUSE is a reason something happens, and the EFFECT is what happens. For example, in the story "Thank You, M'am," a boy wants shoes (cause), so he tries to steal money (effect). He steals money *because* he wants shoes. Read the sentences below. Mark the cause with a C; mark the effect with an E.

1. The boy looked hungry. _____C_____

The woman fed him. _____E_____

2. The strap broke. _____

The boy fell. _____

3. She did not release him. _____

He said he would run. _____

4. She washed his face. _____

His face looked dirty. _____

5. The boy wanted to go. _____

The woman held tight. _____

6. The boy was honest. _____

The woman trusted the boy. _____

7. He dried his face. _____

His face was wet. _____

8. He offered to go to the store. _____

The boy felt guilty. _____

Four Haiku/A Bee Thumps

A HAIKU is a poem that has five syllables in the first and third lines, and seven syllables in the second line.

Create a haiku to accompany this picture. Remember the 5-7-5 pattern.

_____

_____

_____

Choose a haiku from your book and write it on the lines below. Draw a picture to go with it.

_____

_____

_____

Write a second haiku and draw a picture to go with it.

_____

_____

_____

76 PURPLE LEVEL, Unit 4

Starvation Wilderness

Compare/Contrast

Choose from the word list at the bottom of the page. Place things
related to the city in the lefthand column; place things related to
the country in the righthand column. If something can be found in
both places, write it in each column.

CITY	COUNTRY
_____	_____
_____	_____
_____	_____
_____	_____
_____	_____
_____	_____
_____	_____
_____	_____
_____	_____
_____	_____
_____	_____
_____	_____
_____	_____

skyscrapers	mountains	deer	schools
office	buildings	freeway	houses
forests	trees	bears	cars
people	neon lights	subways	creek
visitors	dirt roads	sculptures	museums
birds	log homes	factories	hospital
university	shopping mall		

Starvation Wilderness

Opinions vs. Facts

A FACT is something that can be proven to be true. An OPINION is what someone thinks, and may differ from one person to another.

It is a fact that the temperature is 70°. It is an opinion that 70° is cool.

Determine whether the statements below are facts or opinions. Place an F by a fact; place an O by an opinion.

_____ **1.** The scow was heavy.

_____ **2.** The time was late August of 1922.

_____ **3.** We were in completely unfamiliar territory.

_____ **4.** The west shore was the best place to settle.

_____ **5.** The tent measured 9 x 12 feet.

_____ **6.** The tent was small.

_____ **7.** It was a bitter winter.

_____ **8.** It was too dark for Walter to see.

_____ **9.** It was dangerous.

_____ **10.** We did not see a living thing.

_____ **11.** It took six days to make the trip.

_____ **12.** This is the easiest page in the book.

Starvation Wilderness

A, B, C, D, E, F, G, . . .

Words in a dictionary are arranged in ALPHABETICAL order. Number the words below as they would appear in a dictionary. Remember, if the words start with the same letter, look at the second letter, and so on.

_3_ bird	____ cold	____ faster
_2_ baby	____ disaster	____ hike
_1_ apple	____ deer	____ far
_4_ chair	____ cabin	____ frozen
		____ heavy

____ ammunition	____ knife
____ broth	____ ice
____ blankets	____ hooks
____ baby	____ handles
____ breakfast	____ jackfish

____ rabbits	____ snowshoes
____ pair	____ toboggan
____ muskrat	____ sugar
____ past	____ tea
____ pelts	____ tent
	____ steamboat
	____ skunk

____ weasels

____ zero

____ wilderness

____ winter

Three Poems

Late Date, Fat Cat, Horse Course

RHYMING words are words that *sound* alike. An example of two words that rhyme is cat/bat. Rhyming words aren't always spelled alike. An example is wait/gate.

Can you place the letter of the rhyming word next to each word on the left?

_____	**1.** dreams		**a.**	brings
_____	**2.** sell		**b.**	tree
_____	**3.** horse		**c.**	date
_____	**4.** sold		**d.**	jail
_____	**5.** sings		**e.**	cast
_____	**6.** yield		**f.**	down
_____	**7.** die		**g.**	sat
_____	**8.** pail		**h.**	seems
_____	**9.** walked		**i.**	token
_____	**10.** free		**j.**	field
_____	**11.** wait		**k.**	course
_____	**12.** wanted		**l.**	sea
_____	**13.** crown		**m.**	bell
_____	**14.** sore		**n.**	go
_____	**15.** broken		**o.**	boy
_____	**16.** fast		**p.**	lie
_____	**17.** snow		**q.**	haunted
_____	**18.** joy		**r.**	tore
_____	**19.** three		**s.**	talked
_____	**20.** rat		**t.**	hold

Three Poems

You are the Poet

On the lines below, write a poem about the country you were born in. Make the last word in some of the lines rhyme. Use the space above to illustrate your poem.

TITLE: _____

_____

_____

_____

_____

_____

_____

_____

Amigo Brothers

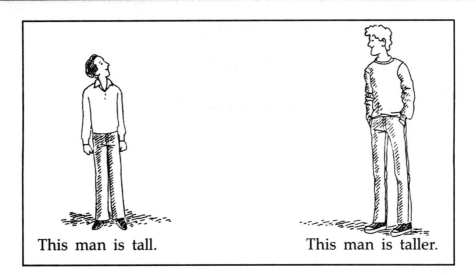

This man is tall.   This man is taller.

I. When comparing two people or things, the suffix -er is added to an adjective to make it comparative. When adjective ends in y, change the y to i before adding er, as in happy-happier and angry-angrier. Make these adjectives comparative by adding the suffix -er.

ADJECTIVE	COMPARATIVE FORM
fair	_____
lean	_____
lanky*	_____
dark	_____
husky*	_____
small	_____
fancy*	_____
short	_____
heavy	_____
quick	_____

*Did you change the y to i?

II. Write three sentences using some of these adjectives.

_____

_____

_____

Name _____ Date _____

Amigo Brothers

Compare/Contrast

I. Compare and contrast Antonio and Felix by writing different qualities in the outside portions of the circles, and by writing similar qualities in the center portion of the circle.

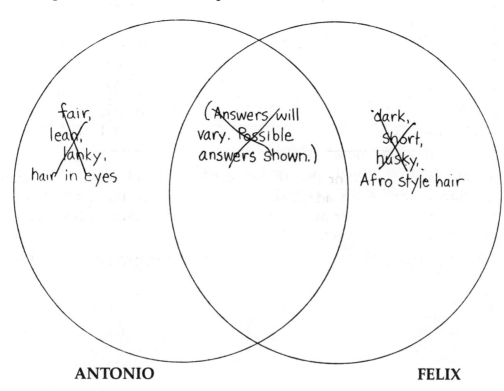

fair, lean, lanky, hair in eyes

(Answers will vary. Possible answers shown.)

dark, short, husky, Afro style hair

ANTONIO   FELIX

II. Now write three to five sentences comparing the two friends.

_____

_____

_____

_____

_____

On the Ledge

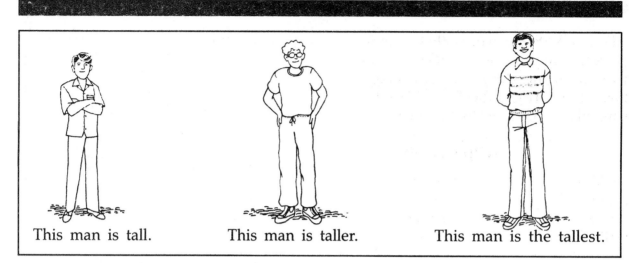

This man is tall.   This man is taller.   This man is the tallest.

I. When comparing three or more people or things, the suffix -est is added to an adjective to make it superlative. Make these adjectives superlative by adding the suffix -est.

ADJECTIVE	SUPERLATIVE FORM
white	_____
soft	_____
tight	_____
young	_____
smart	_____
damp	_____
light	_____
old	_____
strong	_____
calm	_____

II. Write three to five sentences using the superlative form of the adjectives.

e.g. 1. This is the whitest snow I have ever seen.

    2. _____

    3. _____

    4. _____

    5. _____

On The Ledge

ADJECTIVES are words that describe people, places, things, or ideas. Below are some adjectives from the story "On The Ledge." Can you place the correct adjective in front of the person, place, or thing in the story?

ADJECTIVES

shaking	burning	young
rough	wet	red
tanned	narrow	phone
sixth-floor	strong	sticky

_____ bricks   _____ shirt

_____ face   _____ ledge   _____ man

_____ fire truck   _____ sun   _____ wind

_____ hand   _____ book   _____ forehead

                                 _____ window

Choose two of the phrases and use them in your own sentences.

_____

_____

_____

PURPLE LEVEL, Unit 4 **85**

On The Ledge

Read the following statements related to the story "On The Ledge." Decide which statements are reasons that Sergeant Gray wanted to help Walter. Mark these statements with an X.

_____ **1.** Sergeant Gray had a son Walter's age.

_____ **2.** Policeman should help people who are in danger.

_____ **3.** Walter was brave to go out on the ledge.

_____ **4.** Sergeant Gray felt sorry for Walter.

_____ **5.** Walter's shirt was wet.

_____ **6.** If Walter jumped, he might hurt someone below.

_____ **7.** Gray liked climbing on window ledges.

Now, *you* give a reason Sergeant Gray wanted to help Walter.

_____

Terror in the North

A SYNONYM is a word that means the same as another word. Some examples of synonyms are *big/large* and *hard/difficult*. The words below are from the story "Terror in the North." See if you can match each synonym, or word that means the same.

_____ **1.** courageous   **a.** baby

_____ **2.** stress   **b.** difficulty

_____ **3.** problem   **c.** brave

_____ **4.** town   **d.** pressure

_____ **5.** infant   **e.** noise

_____ **6.** sound   **f.** shaking

_____ **7.** trembling   **g.** city

_____ **8.** terrible   **h.** awful

_____ **9.** tremendous   **i.** great

     PURPLE LEVEL, Unit 5   **87**

Terror in the North

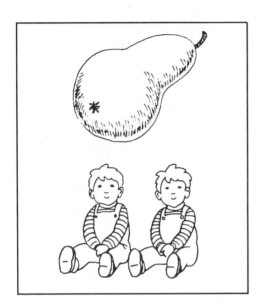

HOMONYMS are words that sound alike, but have different meanings and are spelled differently. Underline the correct word in the sentences below. The first one has been done for you.

1. Few people really (no, know) how they will behave under stress.

2. Seward was scheduled to receive the award in (one, won) (weak, week).

3. She had arrived to live with her (aunt, ant) and uncle.

4. Her blonde hair, (blue, blew) eyes and (fair, fare) skin took at least (to, too, two) years off her 16.

5. Stina truly enjoyed being (their, there, they're).

6. She began looking (threw, through) a magazine.

7. Her (whole, hole) body felt tense.

8. I don't mean to (seem, seam) unfriendly.

9. She looked (passed, past) (hymn, him).

10. I've got to get out of (hear, here).

11. It couldn't (be, bee) (reel, real).

12. There was nothing to (do dew) (but, butt) (wait, weight).

Terror in the North

An ANTONYM is a word that means the opposite of another word. Some examples of antonyms are *short/tall* and *big/little*. See if you can match the pairs of antonyms below by writing the letter from a word in Column B next to a word in Columm A.

COLUMN A

_____f_____ **1.** few

_____ **2.** close

_____ **3.** south

_____ **4.** slender

_____ **5.** quiet

_____ **6.** powerful

_____ **7.** beneath

_____ **8.** last

_____ **9.** night

_____ **10.** shouted

COLUMN B

a. weak

b. north

c. heavy

d. day

e. first

f. many

g. noisy

h. far

i. above

j. whispered

The Secret Life of Walter Mitty

An ADVERB is a word that describes a verb, or action word. Some examples are: The girl sang *sweetly*. The bird *quickly* flew. Adverbs tell how something was done. Many adverbs end with the suffix -ly. Look at the words is parentheses below. Add -ly to each one to make an adverb that will fit into the sentence. Write the word.

(aimless) He drove _____.

(slow) Walter drove _____.

(gross) She seemed _____ unfamiliar.

(delicate) He began fingering _____ the dials.

(nervous) Renshaw spoke _____.

(close) The attendant looked at Walter Mitty _____.

(cautious) He _____ backed out of the lane.

(expert) Mitty examined it _____.

(savage) The District Attorney struck at her _____.

(careless) "A bit of a near thing," said Captain Mitty _____.

The Secret Life of Walter Mitty

An ADJECTIVE is a word that describes a noun, or a person, place, thing, or idea. Some examples are: The *gray* sky threatened rain. *Old* and *helpless*, the woman looked sad. In the sentences below, all of the nouns have been capitalized. Can you find the adjectives that describe each of the nouns? Underline them.

1. She seemed like a <u>strange</u> WOMAN.

2. You're not a young MAN any longer.

3. A door opened down a long, cool CORRIDOR.

4. McMillan was a millionaire BANKER and a close personal FRIEND.

5. It was huge, complicated MACHINE.

6. The two SPECIALISTS had grave, uncertain FACES.

7. He hated these weekly TRIPS to town.

8. An excited BUZZ ran around the courtroom.

9. He wore his right ARM in a sling.

10. I want some BISCUITS for small, young DOGS.

11. The greatest pistol SHOT in the word thought for a moment.

The Secret Life of Walter Mitty

I. A CONTRACTION is a word formed by combining two words. Examples of common contractions are ISN'T (is not), CAN'T (can not), and DIDN'T (did not). An apostrophe (') is used to show where letters have been left out. Can you write the correct contraction to the right of each set of words below? Choose from the contractions at the bottom of the page. Cross off each word as you use it.

can not = can't   has not = _____   you will = _____

    we are = _____

    it will = _____

    I will = _____

    they will = _____

    would not = _____

    could not = _____

    will not = _____

    he will = _____

    we will = _____

    should not = _____

    I would = _____

    he is = _____

    she is = _____

    it is = _____

    was not = _____

    she will = _____

    they are = _____

    are not = _____

wasn't	won't	couldn't	wouldn't
she'll	he'll	they'll	they're
we'll	we're	aren't	I'll
it's	it'll	hasn't	you'll
she's	he's	I'd	shouldn't

II. Use at least five of these contractions in sentences.

1. _____

2. _____

3. _____

4. _____

5. _____

I Have a Dream

Your school is having elections for student body officers. You have decided to run for office. In five sentences, tell which office you are running for, and convince us why we should vote for you.

_____

_____

_____

_____

_____

_____

_____

_____

I Have a Dream

Martin Luther King, Jr. had a dream that all people would be free and equal. What is your dream for a better world? Your dream might involve your family, your neighborhood, the United States, or the entire world. Tell about your dream below. Begin with the words "I have a dream . . ."

Ulysses and the Trojan Horse

A COMPOUND WORD is a word that has been formed by combining two smaller words. The words "cook" and "book" combine to form the word "cookbook." "Book" and "end" combine to form "bookend."

The words below are all compound words from the story "Ulysses and the Trojan Horse." Next to each compuond word, write the two smaller words that were combined.

1. grapevine = _____grape_____ + _____vine_____

2. daybreak = _____ + _____

3. blacksmith = _____ + _____

4. shopkeeper = _____ + _____

5. peacetime = _____ + _____

6. anything = _____ + _____

7. standstill = _____ + _____

8. rooftop = _____ + _____

9. moonbeam = _____ + _____

10. something = _____ + _____

11. tonight = _____ + _____

Ulysses and the Trojan Horse

An ADJECTIVE is a word that describes a person, place, thing, or idea. Think of some adjectives that describe Ulysses. Write them below.

Use the words in sentences about Ulysses.

_____

_____

_____

_____

Ulysses Meets the Cyclops

A SIMILE uses the words "like" or "as" to compare two things. The phrase "pretty as a picture" is comparing a girl's beauty to a picture.

See if you can identify the similes below from the story "Ulysses Meets the Cyclops." Underline the two things that are being compared in each simile.

1. He looked like a hairy mountain.

2. His hands caught two of my friends like squealing puppies.

3. He gobbled the meat like a hungry lion.

4. he did it as easily as you'd stick the stopper in a bottle.

5. The log was as long and thick as the mast of my ship.

6. It was as tough as iron.

7. I twirled it till it was spinning like a drill.

8. Our sadness was as large as the ocean.

Name _____ Date _____

Ulysses Meets the Cyclops

A PRONOUN is a word that takes the place of a common or proper noun. In the sentence "He went to the store," the word "he" might take the place of "the boy" or "Tom." Other pronouns are: he, she, we, it, you, us, them, I, her, him, they. Replace the nouns below with an appropriate pronoun. (The nouns have been underlined.) Write the new sentence.

1. The Cyclops was still out with his sheep.

   _____

2. His men crowded around Ulysses.

   _____

3. The Cyclops came back with his flock.

   _____

4. Ulysses and his men thrust the spear into the fire.

   _____

5. The name had fooled the Cyclops!

   _____

6. This Nobody won't get out of here alive!

   _____

7. Ulysses and his men had lost their friends.

   _____

8. Sue is done with this page.

   _____

Andre/Family Album

Synonyms are similiar. Write a synonym for each of the following words. Use a dictionary or thesaurus if you need help.

1. orderly   _____
2. horrors   _____
3. simple   _____
4. precise   _____
5. difficult   _____
6. casual   _____
7. construct   _____
8. explore   _____
9. astounded   _____
10. special   _____
11. conclusion   _____
12. rare   _____
13. report   _____
14. bright   _____
15. ready   _____
16. triumphantly   _____
17. defensive   _____
18. independence   _____

Choose seven of the synomys and use in a sentence.

1. The room was very orderly. _____

2. _____

3. _____

4. _____

5. _____

6. _____

7. _____

Name _____ Date _____

Bread

In the following paragraph, circle the contractions. On the blank following the paragraph, write the pronoun and the verb that each contraction represents.

We're planning a camping trip to the Colorado Rockies this spring. We think it's a great experience to sleep in tents under the beautiful night sky. Our teacher taught us what we will need to know to go on this trip. He's explained how to use a knife and how to build a campfire. It'll be very exciting. We've heard about the fun of riding the rapids in a raft.

_____ _____ _____ _____ _____

Choose five of the following contractions and write five sentences using your choices. I'll   he'd   she'll   we'd   it's   they're   You'll

1. _____

2. _____

3. _____

4. _____

5. _____

Name _____ Date _____

Somebody's Son

Choose the correct form in each of the following sentences and write it in the space at the right.

1. Beside the house (stand, stands) a pine tree and an oak tree. _____

2. Either you or Peter (is, are) going to the science fair. _____

3. Math (was, were) Jeff's favorite subject.

_____

4. Both Mary and John (sings, sing) beautifully.

_____

5. Under the table (is, are) the missing toy.

_____

6. A picture of my family (is, are) hanging on the wall. _____

7. I shall be happy if either Lynn or Cindy (decide, decides) the date of the party.

_____

8. Tom failed the test because the spelling on his essays (was, were) so bad. _____

9. There (isn't, aren't) many students at school this late. _____

10. Neither Chuck nor Mark (insists, insist) on going to the movies every week.

_____

11. Both of the suspects (maintains, maintain) that they are innocent.

_____

12. Every one of his stories (seems, seem) to please the entire class.

_____

13. A basket of fruit (was, were) on the kitchen table. _____

14. Diamonds (is, are) my favorite gem. _____

15. (Do, does) Mike and Tony intend to go to the game? _____

102 **PURPLE LEVEL, Unit 5**

Name _____ Date _____

Somebody's Son

The following are pairs of homophones. Homophones are words
that sound alike but have different spellings and different meanings.
Use each of the pairs in a sentence to show that you understand
the difference.

1. pain - pane   **6.** great - grate

2. soul - sole   **7.** four - for

3. night - knight   **8.** would - wood

4. sail - sale   **9.** see - sea

5. our - hour   **10.** eight - ate

1. _____

_____

2. _____

_____

3. _____

_____

4. _____

_____

5. _____

_____

6. _____

_____

7. _____

_____

8. _____

_____

9. _____

_____

10. _____

_____

Medicine Bag

Negative prefixes are un, dis, il, ir, and im. These prefixes mean not. Underline the negative prefix and write the root word on the line provided for the following words.

1. impossible   _____
2. unhappy   _____
3. disagreeable   _____
4. illogical   _____
5. irrational   _____
6. dissatisfied   _____
7. irresponsible   _____
8. unthinkable   _____
9. unspoken   _____
10. unacceptable   _____
11. immature   _____
12. immovable   _____
13. disapprove   _____
14. disrespect   _____
15. illegible   _____

Choose seven of the words above and use each in a sentence.

1. _____

2. _____

3. _____

4. _____

5. _____

6. _____

7. _____

Medicine/Grandfather

In the following sentences circle the adjectives. The number of adjectives is noted at the end of each sentence. The first sentence is done for you.

1. The beautiful woman sitting behind the antique desk is my sister. (2)
2. Tod began the grueling marathon. (1)
3. My grades are excellent. (1)
4. The daring thief dashed down the dark, silent street. (3)
5. He was an intelligent man. (1)
6. The weather is warm. (1)
7. A beautiful rainbow appeared after the terrible storm. (2)
8. The child had a happy face and a cheerful disposition. (2)
9. Corinne is a fine actress and an adequate dancer. (2)
10. The entire valley was hidden in the dense fog. (2)
11. A quick jog is an excellent way to keep in good shape. (3)
12. The tiny dog barked at the noisy children. (2)
13. Tom was a fantastic leader and a good friend. (2)
14. They gave their old clothes to the poor. (1)
15. The elegant woman was dressed in a blue suit. (2)
16. Two old men stood on the windswept cliff. (3)
17. A large number of students did not pass the last important test. (3)

Some People/My People

Write the adjectives and adverbs under the correct column to the left of the sentences. The first has been done for you.

Adjectives	Adverbs	
young	quickly	**1.** The young teacher collected our papers quickly.
_____	_____	**2.** We closely watched as she place the thick stack on the desk.
_____	_____	**3.** The quiet class noticed that she momentarily glanced out the window.
_____	_____	**4.** As we carefully watched she lifted the new book from the desk.
_____	_____	**5.** We knew we would shortly start a new adventure.
_____	_____	**6.** Amazingly, we looked forward to this interesting project.
_____	_____	**7.** We learned next day that we would nearly be through the chapter.
_____	_____	**8.** Enthusiastically, we tackled the short chapter
_____	_____	**9.** Later, the difficult homework was assigned.

Some People/My People

Complete the sentence below to create hyperboles. Use these words:
bucket, truck, steam, sky, teacher, mile, star, elephant, ears, and
rock.

1. I'm so hungry that I could eat an

   _____.

2. Make me a sandwich a _____

   high.

3. I am so sad, I could cry a

   _____ful of tears.

4. The pizza was so large, we had to bring it

   home in a _____.

5. His father was so angry, _____

   came out of his ears.

6. The rock group was so loud, our

   _____ fell off.

7. The stale bread is hard as a

   _____.

8. The play was so bad, the _____

   went home.

9. The class was so boring, the _____ fell asleep.

10. I jumped so high, I touched the _____.

Use the following phrases to write your own hyperboles. Be sure to
exaggerate.

1. It snowed so hard _____

2. I ate so much _____

3. He was so frightened _____

4. It was so cold _____

Name _____ Date _____

Identify each underlined word in the following sentences as either a
noun or a verb. Place you answers on the lines provided at the end
of each sentence.

1. Terry's car runs smoothly. _____

   _____

2. Two dogs played on the front porch.

   _____ _____

3. The drapes in the living room were torn.

   _____ _____

4. The Mustang belongs to Charlie.

   _____

5. Give me your correct address.

   _____ _____

6. Mary and Sue bought tickets for the

   concert. _____ _____

7. Nobody wanted the play to end.

   _____ _____

8. Behind the house was a swing.

   _____ _____

9. All the musicians had long hair. _____ _____ _____

10. The hotel stands on top of the mountain. _____ _____

11. We recognized the woman from the old photograph. _____

   _____ _____

12. The election proved that Dan was the winner. _____ _____

13. We will drive for at least eight hours before we get to the mountains.

   _____ _____ _____

14. Your answer was the first correct one. _____ _____

15. Jane was sitting on the top rail of the corral. _____ _____

   _____ _____

Name _____ Date _____

Whale Hunting/Luther Leavitt

Personification is a figure of speech that gives human characteristics to objects, animals, or abstract ideas. Example: The dishes glared at me from the sink.

In each blank below, write the letter of the word that would create personification for the word or phrase.

a. danced   **c.** screamed   **e.** whistled   **g.** chewed
b. crawled   **d.** groaned   **f.** cried   **h.** sang

— garbage disposal   — the chair   — fog   — wind chimes
— the wind   — the candlelight   — the rain clouds   — sirens

Write the sentences for five of the matching pairs.

Example: The garbage disposal chewed up the old bones.

1. _____

2. _____

3. _____

4. _____

5. _____